Safari park

Tessa Krailing

Nelson

Contents

On safari

One day, Rocky came home from school.
He was very excited.
'Mum,' he called as he rushed through
the front door.
'What is it?' asked Mrs Rockwell.
'Our class is going on a
trip on Saturday,' said Rocky.
'It's a trip to a safari park.
We have to take the money to school tomorrow.'
Rocky's Mum looked at the note Rocky had
brought home from school.
'Sorry, Rocky,' she said.
'I haven't got enough money.
You won't be able to go.'

WATERLOO SCHOOL

Trip to Safari Park

Saturday 20th March

The school bus leaves

Rocky was fed up but he didn't say
anything to his Mum.
He knew if she had the money she
would let him go.
He tried not to show he was upset
about missing the trip.

Saturday soon came.
Rocky didn't have to go to school but
went over there to see the others
go off in the bus.
When they had gone, Rocky walked back
to the Square.
There was no-one at home because his Mum
had gone to work so he went into the park.

He was sitting on a park bench looking
very fed up when Mr Keeping walked by.
'What's wrong?' he asked Rocky.
Rocky told him about the trip to the
safari park.
'Never mind,' said Mr Keeping.
'We have our own safari park right here.'

Rocky looked surprised.
'A safari park has wild animals,'
said Mr Keeping.
'Well, there are wild animals in
Wellington Square. Follow me.'

Rocky got up and followed Mr Keeping around
the park.
'Look,' said Mr Keeping. 'There's a hedgehog.'
And Mr Keeping pointed.
'And here's a ladybird. Watch carefully.
We might see it open its wings.'
'That's OK,' said Rocky, 'but it's not
like a real safari park.
For a start there aren't any lions.
There aren't any dangerous animals in
Wellington Square.'

'All right,' said Mr Keeping. 'You wait here.
I'll be back in a minute.'
Mr Keeping came back with a tent.
'We'll make it like a real safari,' he said.
'Help me put up the tent.'
When the tent was up, Mr Keeping and
Rocky sat down in front of it.
'Now,' said Mr Keeping.
'This isn't Wellington Square.
This is Africa. You are on safari in Africa.
Get inside the tent.
I'll lend you my camera.
You always have a camera on safari to take
pictures of all the wild animals you see.'

Rocky sat inside the tent.
He thought about the other kids in a
real safari park.
He wished he was with them.
Mr Keeping was trying to cheer him up but
Wellington Square just wasn't a safari park.

Suddenly, Fred stuck his head through
the flap in the tent.
'What's going on?' he asked.
'Why have you put up this tent in my park?'
'I'm on safari,' said Rocky.
'I'm in Africa looking for wild animals.'
'Oh,' said Fred and left Rocky to his game.

Mr Keeping came back with the camera.
'Now, take some good pictures of all the
wild animals you see,' he said.
Rocky sat in the tent for a few minutes.
Nothing happened.
He was just thinking about going home to
watch television when he heard a noise.

The flap of the tent moved a little and
Rocky saw a snake coming in.
At first he was scared, but then he saw
that it was only Bruce.
He laughed.
Bruce was Mr Keeping's pet snake.

The leopard

Ten minutes later Mr Keeping came back.
'I've brought you something to eat,' he said.
'Oh, thanks,' said Rocky taking the pork pie and
crisps that Mr Keeping had brought.
'And thanks for lending me Bruce.
He gave me a fright!'
'Did you use the camera?' asked Mr Keeping.
'No,' said Rocky. 'I forgot.'
'Well, remember next time you see a wild animal.
I'd better take Bruce back home now.'

Rocky sat in the tent and ate the crisps and
some of the pork pie.
Suddenly, he saw a shadow on the tent.
It was the shadow of a cat.
A very, very, very big cat.
Rocky sat very still.
What was Mr Keeping up to now?
The shadow moved round to the front of the tent.
Suddenly, a cat stuck its head through
the flap in the tent.
But it wasn't like any other cat.
It had brown spots all over its coat.
It was a leopard!

Rocky moved to the back of the tent.
The leopard came in and began eating what
was left of Rocky's pork pie.
At first Rocky was scared but then he thought,
'Mr Keeping must have brought the leopard.
I'd better take a picture.'
He reached for the camera but then
he had another thought,
'Mr Keeping doesn't have a leopard!'

Rocky was really scared now.
He was trapped in the tent.
The leopard finished the pork pie and
lay down next to Rocky. It fell asleep.
Rocky kept very still.
He was afraid to move but he knew he
had to get away.

He started to move very slowly.
He crawled along, being careful not to
touch the leopard.
Could he get away before the leopard woke up?
The leopard was still asleep as Rocky quickly
threw himself through the flap in the tent.

When he was outside he rushed over to
where Fred was working.
'Fred! Fred!' he shouted.
'There's a leopard in my tent!'
Fred smiled.
'Well, well, a leopard, eh?
You do see leopards on safari.'

'It's true,' said Rocky.
'I know you don't believe me, but come with me
and you'll see!'
Fred and Rocky walked over to the tent.
'There really IS a leopard in my tent,'
said Rocky.
'He's asleep, so we'd better be quiet.'

They went quietly to the front of the tent and
Rocky carefully pulled back the flap.
The tent was empty!
'Where?' said Fred.
'Where's the leopard?
I don't see any leopard!'
'But it WAS here,' said Rocky.
'It ate my pork pie and then it fell asleep.'
Fred laughed.
'You're pulling my leg,' he said.
'I almost believed you for a minute.
That was a good joke!'
Fred was still laughing as he went back
to his weeding.

Where is the leopard?

Rocky left the park and went to
Mr Keeping's house.
He knocked on the door.
He told Mr Keeping about the leopard but
Mr Keeping thought it was a joke too.
Rocky wished he'd taken a picture
of the leopard.
Then people would have to believe him.

Rocky went back to the park.
'I WILL find that leopard,' he said to himself.
'I'll go and get the camera so when I see it
I can take a picture.
Then Fred and Mr Keeping will believe me.'

He went back to the tent.
He lifted the flap carefully and looked in.
The leopard had not come back.
Rocky picked up the camera and walked around
the park looking for the leopard.

'Looking for something?' asked PC Kent.

Rocky jumped.

He hadn't seen the policeman come up behind him.

'Yes,' he said. 'I'm looking for a leopard.'

PC Kent laughed.

'Don't look too hard.

You'll get spots before your eyes!'

'It's not a joke,' said Rocky.

'The leopard came into my tent and
ate my pork pie.

It's somewhere in the park and I'm going
to find it.'

'What you saw was just a big cat,' said PC Kent.

'You won't find a leopard in Wellington Square.'

'I will find it,' said Rocky.

'And when I do I'll take a picture.'

'I'd like to see that,' said PC Kent as
he walked away.

'How can I find the leopard?' thought Rocky.
'I know! I'll go and get Max.
He's good at finding cats.'

Rocky went home.
Max was really pleased to see him.
He jumped up and down excitedly and
wagged his tail.
'Good dog,' said Rocky.
'Now, come on. I've got a job for you to do.
You have to find a cat for me.
A very big cat with brown spots on its coat.'

Rocky took Max over to the park.
'Now, Max, find the cat!'
Max ran about and then he stopped suddenly
by Fred's shed.
He had come face to face with the leopard.

But Rocky didn't see what Max had found.
He was watching the other kids coming over to the
park.
They had come back from the trip.

Ben and the others came over to the fence.
'We had a great time,' said Ben.
'We saw chimps and lions and lots of other
dangerous animals.'
'I had a ride on an elephant,' said Jamila.
'We were sorry you couldn't come with us,'
said Tony.
'Oh,' said Rocky. 'I had a great time too.
I went on safari in Wellington Square.
A leopard came into my tent.'
The other kids laughed.
'A leopard?' said Ben.
'Did you have an elephant in your tent as well?'
'It's true,' said Rocky.
'There really was a leopard!'
'Sure,' said Tony, 'there are lots of leopards
in Wellington Square.'

The kids walked off talking about their trip.
They soon forgot Rocky and his silly joke
about the leopard.
So Rocky just gave the tent back to Mr Keeping and
went home to tea.

Hunt the leopard

That night Rocky couldn't sleep.
He had told his Mum about the leopard but
she hadn't believed him.
No-one had believed him.
They all thought it was a joke.
Rocky began to think that he hadn't seen
the leopard at all!

Early the next morning, Rocky heard
his Mum calling.
'Rocky, come downstairs quickly.
Come and look at the newspaper.'

Rocky rushed downstairs and looked at
the newspaper with his Mum.
There was a picture of a leopard and a lady.
Rocky's Mum read out what it said.
'POLICE IN HUNT FOR RAMONA'S LEOPARD
Yesterday, lovely Ramona Rome lost
her pet leopard, Spot.
The police believe it is somewhere near
Wellington Square. Watch out!
If you see the leopard don't go near it,
but tell the police at once.'

'I knew I'd seen a real leopard,' said Rocky.
Just then there was a knock on the door.
Rocky opened the door.
'Good morning, Rocky,' said PC Kent.
'About that leopard you said you saw yesterday.
Well, it looks as if you were telling the truth.
Have you seen the newspaper?'
'Yes,' said Rocky, 'and I did see the leopard!'
'Will you show me where you saw it?'
asked PC Kent.

Rocky and PC Kent went over to the park.
'It was here,' said Rocky.
'This is where the tent was.
I went to get Fred and when we came back
the leopard had gone.'
'Well, it could have gone a long way by now,'
said PC Kent.
'We'll just have to keep looking.'

All the kids came out to look for the leopard.
'I wish I'd seen the leopard,' said Kevin.
'I wish I hadn't gone to the safari park.
We only saw a few old lions.
We should have stayed here and seen the leopard.'

'Be careful,' said Mr Keeping.
'If you see the leopard don't go up to it.
We don't know how wild it is.
It might be dangerous.'

While the kids were looking for the leopard,
a big black car pulled up in front of the park.
A lady got out and came into the park.
'That's Ramona Rome,' said Rocky.
'Her picture was in the paper this morning.'
A man with a camera walked over to her.
'I'm a reporter from the newspaper,' he said.
'Can you tell me anything about
the missing leopard?
Is it dangerous?'
'No,' said Ramona. 'He's not dangerous at all.
He's my darling pet and his name's Spot.
Oh, I do hope they find him soon.'

The reporter took a picture of Ramona.
'Now where's the kid who saw the leopard?'
he asked.
Rocky came over.
'I saw the leopard,' he said.
'Great!' said the reporter.
'I want a picture of you too.'

When the reporter had taken the pictures,
everyone began to look for the leopard again.
They called out 'Spot!' and looked all over
the park but they didn't see the big cat.
Suddenly, Rocky said, 'Where's Fred?
I haven't seen him all morning.'

Fred finds the leopard

PC Kent went over to Fred's shed and
the others followed him.
'Fred, are you in there?' he called.
'Help!' shouted Fred. 'Someone help!'
'I'd better go in,' said PC Kent.
'Stand well back, everyone.'

PC Kent slowly opened the door of the shed.
Fred was sitting on a bench with his
back to the wall.
At his feet lay Spot the leopard.
'About time too,' said Fred when he saw PC Kent.
'I've been stuck in here all night with
this dangerous animal.
Will you please take it away!'

'He's not dangerous,' said Ramona.
'He won't hurt you.
Come here, Spot, here, darling boy.'
The leopard got up and went over to Ramona.
'Is it safe?' asked Rocky.
'He's quite safe,' said Ramona, 'but I'd better
keep him on a chain.'
'Make sure you do,' said PC Kent.

Next morning Rocky rushed downstairs to
look at the newspaper.
His picture was on the front and there
was one of Ramona and Spot.
'Look, Mum!' he shouted. 'There's a picture of me!'
Rocky read out loud to his Mum.
'ROCKY SPOTS RAMONA'S SPOT!'
'No-one believed me,' said Rocky, 'not until
they all saw the leopard.'
'Seeing is believing!' said his Mum.